KU-297-385

Don't Tell Anyone, But...

Written by Susie Linn

Illustrated by Erika Meza

TOP THAT

Licensed exclusively to Top That Publishing Ltd
Tide Mill Way, Woodbridge, Suffolk, IP12 1AP, UK
www.topthatpublishing.com
Copyright © 2016 Tide Mill Media
All rights reserved
0 2 4 6 8 9 7 5 3 1
Manufactured in China

All rights reserved. No part of this publication may be reproduced, stored in a retrieval system, or transmitted in any form or by any means, electronic, mechanical, photocopying, recording or otherwise, without the prior written permission of the publisher. Neither this book nor any part or any of the illustrations, photographs or reproductions contained in it shall be sold or disposed of otherwise than as a complete book, and any unauthorised sale of such part illustration, photograph or reproduction shall be deemed to be a breach of the publisher's copyright.

ISBN 978-1-78445-590-3

A catalogue record for this book is available from the British Library

'Don't tell anyone, but ... this one's for you, G.'

Squirrel was excited. She hopped and skipped and twitched her bushy tail with excitement! She had a secret – and she had to share it with someone.

The very first 'someone' she saw was Rabbit.

Rabbit was busy looking for the greenest, tastiest patches of grass, so she took a quick look at Squirrel and carried on with her search. Squirrel lowered her voice and whispered ...

'Don't tell anyone, but ...
I'm having a big party
with yummy food and
funny hats!'

'Oh ... really?' mumbled Rabbit, who was far more interested in her
delicious grass. She wasn't listening properly to Squirrel at all!

So when Rabbit spotted her friend, Mole, who was busy digging, she had some rather strange news. In hushed tones, Rabbit whispered in Mole's velvety ear …

'Don't tell anyone, but ... Squirrel's having a party and she's inviting lots of stray cats!'

'Hmmm ... I see,' muttered Mole, as he inspected his newly-dug hole. He wasn't paying much attention to Rabbit!

Later, Mole spied his friend, Fox, basking in the autumn sun, and decided to tell him the news. He scampered over and said ...

'Don't tell anyone, but ...
Squirrel's having a picnic
and she's making pies for
all the rats.'

'Zzzz ... whatever ...' snored Fox, lazily.
He was far more interested in catching the last rays
of sunshine and had only half heard Mole's news.

As day turned to dusk,
Fox saw his friend, Owl, perching
in an oak tree, waiting for the
moon to appear.

'I might as well tell him the news,'
thought Fox, who was more awake by now.
So he walked over to Owl and quietly called up to him ...

'Don't tell anyone, but ...
Squirrel's having a picnic
and she's going to wear
her fancy pants!'

'Well ... there's a thing!'
hooted Owl, paying more
attention to the moon than
to what Fox was saying.

Later, as dawn was breaking, Owl spotted his friend, Deer. He was busy picking his way gracefully through the undergrowth, looking for tasty autumn berries.

'Come here, Deer!' called Owl softly, and as Deer half-turned to him, he lowered his voice and said ...

'Don't tell anyone, but ... Squirrel has a pink stick, to tap with when she learns to dance!'

Deer stopped for a second and looked up in surprise, then he turned back to a particularly juicy crop of blackberries. He hadn't quite caught everything that Owl had said.

That afternoon, Deer bumped
into his friend, Mouse, who was
scurrying around in the leaves.
He was very busy eating the berries
that Deer had dropped.

'Owl told me the strangest thing,'
Deer murmured ...

'Don't tell anyone, but ...
Squirrel's wearing lipstick
and she's gone to tea
with all her aunts!'

Mouse was very hungry indeed – and he certainly wasn't in
the mood for paying much attention to woodland chit-chat.

But when Mouse heard his friend,
Woodpecker, rat-a-tat-tatting
on an old oak tree, he thought
he had better pass on the news.

'If you can spare a minute! ...' he
shouted, to make himself heard
above Woodpecker's noise.

Woodpecker looked down and
Mouse continued at the top
of his little voice ...

'Don't tell anyone, but ...
Squirrel's buying a boat
ticket, to sail the sea to
sunny France!'

But Woodpecker
hadn't entirely stopped
rat-a-tat-tatting, so the
message he thought he
heard was quite different.

'What? Really?! Squirrel's won a prize ...
a lucky chance?' exclaimed
Woodpecker, loudly.

Squirrel had been busy,
minding her own business,
but when she heard
Woodpecker's news,
she jumped up!

'STOP!
LISTEN!
You've got it wrong!'
she called in frustration.

At that, all the creatures stopped what they were doing and looked up.

'It's not true!'
cried Squirrel.

'What ... you haven't had a lucky chance?' asked Woodpecker.

'No, I'm afraid not!' replied Squirrel.

'But you ARE sailing to sunny France ... aren't you?' enquired Mouse.

'No, not ever!' Squirrel declared.

'What about wearing lipstick ... and having tea with your aunts?' tried Deer.

'Absolutely NOT!' cried Squirrel.

'So ... no dancing with a pink stick, then?' hesitated Owl.

'Goodness ... no!' sighed Squirrel, impatiently.

'And you're not having a party with stray cats?' Rabbit whispered.

'No, no, NO ...' Squirrel groaned.

'But what IS happening is that I'm having a big party with *yummy* food and funny hats! And you're all invited!'

The very next day, everyone gathered in the
woodland clearing for Squirrel's big party ...
and they all wore funny hats
and had the best time ever.